It's Where You Finish
That Counts

It's Where You Finish That Counts

The James Russell Story

LEON C. HARRIS

IT'S WHERE YOU FINISH THAT COUNTS
THE JAMES RUSSELL STORY

iUniverse books may be ordered through booksellers or by contacting:

iUniverse
1663 Liberty Drive
Bloomington, IN 47403
www.iuniverse.com
1-800-Authors (1-800-288-4677)

ISBN: 978-1-4917-8231-6 (sc)
ISBN: 978-1-4917-8232-3 (e)

Library of Congress Control Number: 2015918349

Print information available on the last page.

iUniverse rev. date: 11/10/2015

To my wife Diane and to the memory of my parents,
Mildred and Leon Harris, love and gratitude.

The Governor

Chapter 1

The Calling

On a hot, steamy August afternoon, a very excited James Russell entered the law offices of Craig and Russell in downtown Birmingham, Alabama. He had reason to be fired up that day.

Jimmy had just concluded a meeting with one of the most powerful men in Alabama politics. Aside from being one of the richest citizens in the state, Steven Poindexter had been attorney general and lieutenant governor in the early nineties. Poindexter had remained in the Democratic Party even after many of his friends defected to the GOP.

At five foot eleven and weighing almost 180 pounds, he was in great shape. He dressed well, and women swooned over him. He seemed to be permanently tanned and his blue-gray eyes commanded attention. He had been born and raised in Cambridge, Massachusetts.

Why was Jimmy so excited about his lunch date with Poindexter? We could all see the glow in his face when he entered the office that day. He was obviously happy about something.

"Hey, you hit the lottery or something?" asked Sarah Morris, the office secretary.

"Well, it's not every day that a black man, of average means, is asked to run for the governorship of the state of Alabama," Jimmy said. "It floored me when he said the word governor! When someone like Steven Poindexter speaks, you listen. I guess you're wondering what I am talking about." He told us he was happy and scared to death at the same time.

By the way, my name is Larry Ford. I'm a law student and will be an aide to James Russell during his campaign for governor. My minor was language arts, and writing is my favorite pastime. When the attorneys have questions about word choices for briefs or even ads for the papers, they often ask my opinion. What I learned during this time in Alabama history can't even be put into words. You don't get that type of education from a book.

It was exciting, breathtaking, and fearful at the same time. Between my night classes and work at the law office, I had little time for socializing, but God knows I loved every minute of it.

I helped with research for the preparation of briefs, helped set appointments, and answered the phone if necessary. And I ran errands too.

Mr. Russell (I addressed all of the adults respectfully, the way I was taught at home) continued to discuss the day's events. He sat down to explain everything that had transpired at the luncheon. Everyone was happy about the calling, a term jokingly used by Russell's best friend, Horace Craig.

Craig and Jimmy had been roommates at Alabama State, a predominantly black university, and they enrolled in law school around the same time. Unlike Jimmy, Craig worked for the Birmingham Water Works Board instead of beginning a career in teaching.

Among the smiles and congratulations, there was a mix of cautious optimism and foreboding in that room. We all knew there would be excitement and danger if Jimmy took on this challenge. Still, there was reason to celebrate in the office that day, which was a day I'll never forget.

The law office was located in the Civil Rights District of downtown Birmingham. The district includes the Sixteenth Street Baptist Church, where four little girls were killed in a bomb blast on September 15, 1963.

The Civil Rights Institute is located across the street from the historic church. Kelly Ingram Park, where rallies were held during the civil rights demonstrations in the early 1960s, is situated next to those landmarks.

Birmingham has changed a great deal since those days. In the 1960s, the city was a bustling, thriving metropolis with thousands of people employed in the steel industry. The population was nearing four hundred thousand, and the city was growing. Many families depended on the steel industry for their economic security.

The downtown district was a major shopping mecca. People from surrounding counties traveled to Birmingham to shop in the large department stores and dine in the nice restaurants, but black folks were not allowed inside the restaurants in those days.

We learned quite a bit about that period from some of the instructors at the college I attended. Several faculty members were students then and took part in demonstrations during 1962 and 1963. As far as economics was concerned, Birmingham was doing very well.

The Birmingham during Russell's gubernatorial campaign is a different animal. First of all, the steel industry is a mere shadow of what it was then. One of the largest plants, which is located in a section of Birmingham called Ensley, has closed down completely. It had employed hundreds of men and women. The huge plant in Fairfield, a suburb west of Birmingham, had employed thousands, but now it employs around 1,500 people.

The decline in steel production is attributed to the appearance of cheap steel that flooded the market. South Korea, Japan, and China got into the steel-making business during the eighties and nineties. Workers in those countries were paid low wages in some cases, which allowed for cheaper steel prices.

Birmingham has a service-oriented economy today. One of the largest employers is UAB Hospital, and health-related industries in the area employ many more. There are also numerous financial-service businesses in the region.

With the revitalization movement, the "Magic City" is still going through changes. Oh, the city got that nickname because it seemingly sprang up overnight. Some people said it came out of nowhere—as if by magic.

The city's population dropped dramatically during the late eighties and nineties. In addition to white flight, many black families relocated during this trying time. The city is experiencing a slight recovery in population growth. The numbers are not what leaders want to see, but downtown Birmingham is coming back slowly.

The law office was just two blocks from the civil rights district. The office consisted of a small lobby where clients would register and wait for their appointments. Down a narrow hallway, next to a large conference room, was Jimmy's office. His rather small space contained a desk, two straight-backed chairs in front of the desk, and a plant in the corner.

On the wall, to the left of the desk, several shelves contained law books. Jimmy could look out his window and see an alley. To say the room was austere in its appearance would be putting it mildly.

Horace's office was across the hall from the conference room, on the left side of the hallway. It too had only the basic necessities and furnishings. Two tiny offices were located next to Craig's on the left side of the hallway. These offices were occupied by two of the younger attorneys in the firm. The restrooms were at the end of the hallway next to a rear exit. The lawyers in the firm were much more concerned with winning cases than superficial considerations, such as how attractive the offices were. Believe me!

Jimmy had a lot on his plate that day. The very thought of jumping on a stage as huge as the Alabama gubernatorial election campaign was humongous in that country boy's eyes. Alabama was still Alabama, and the same obstacles for a black person seeking statewide office remained. Jimmy loved his state, and anybody trying to put Alabama down would have to deal with him. He made no distinctions about color when speaking of the people who had helped him. Alabama was home, and he didn't even think about living anyplace else.

There were elements in the state who were still clinging to their rigid racist doctrines, but Jimmy believed the majority of white folks in Alabama were good, decent people beneath the façade of racial indifference. He often said, "There are good white folks in Alabama too."

As Russell talked about his meeting, Craig interrupted and asked, "How in the world are you going to swing any white votes in this state, man?"

Mrs. Morris shouted, "You win what you can—where you can!" The secretary's statement might have sounded elementary, but everyone realized that she made a valid point.

I had really enjoyed my political science classes during my undergrad work, but this was real on-the-job training!

I attended Miles College, an HBCU in suburban Fairfield, Alabama. The college has about 2,500 students, is supported by the CME Church, and is a member of the United Negro College Fund. None of my classes there covered this type of drama.

If Jimmy could swing small numbers of white votes in enough places in the state, he might be in contention—if he could capture 98 percent of the black and Hispanic vote. The Hispanic population was increasing steadily, and the Democrats worked that demographic persistently. The plan, if he decided to run, would be to campaign hard throughout the state and win over as many white voters as possible.

Two of the firm's partners were busy at the courthouse. So another meeting was planned to take place at Russell's home that night.

Craig asked Jimmy what his wife thought about the possible run for governor.

"Man, are you kidding? Diane is as fired up as I am," replied Jimmy.

Mr. Russell talked about his wife so much that I could have written a book about her. Mrs. Diane Russell was some woman. She worked her way through college, worked an extra job while her husband was in law school, and raised two great kids. She taught English at the high school for years and then at a community college. Mrs. Russell served as Jimmy's speechwriter when he ran for city council, mayor of Bessemer, and district attorney of Jefferson County. She was a tireless campaigner and fund-raiser. Mrs. Russell was also fiercely loyal to her state. She never forgot what the state had done for her. She told people wherever she traveled that Alabama was the most beautiful state in the country. Most of all, she was a devoted wife and mom. Family was important to "Lady Di," as Jimmy called her.

But first things first. He hadn't even decided to run yet. Jimmy asked Sarah to call his partners at the courthouse. Carey Sutton and Milton Crittenden were to meet at his home at seven o'clock that evening and bring their wives if possible. Fortunately, I was also asked to attend the meeting. The Russells always treated me like a member of the family.

Milton Crittenden was the firm's best litigator, and Jimmy was the firm's best strategist. Horace Craig was outgoing, enthusiastic, and a virtual client magnet. He was the firm's go-getter where business was concerned. Carey Sutton was quiet and studious. Like me, he loved to do research. The two of us were often called on to dig for answers.

The enormity of the task was beginning to sink in, and Jimmy understood the stakes too. He was going to decide that night whether to accept the invitation to seek the Democratic Nomination for governor. He would surround himself with family and friends and ask for their honest opinions. Jimmy called his kids to tell them about the offer, and they would be there too.

Clifton, the older of his two children, was a principal at Curry High School in suburban McCalla, west of Birmingham. Laci Cleveland was a web designer for a Birmingham ad agency.

Since Jimmy's grandchildren would be there also, Mrs. Russell had some monster preparations to handle.

Mrs. Russell's sister, Marsha, Who lived in Hoover, a suburb south of Birmingham, came early to help with preparations.

You might have guessed that Sister Morris pitched in to help too.

***

The Russell home was located in Pelham, a suburb in Shelby County, south of Birmingham. That night, it was full of excitement and joy. And there was some apprehension too. We all waited for Jimmy to speak.

Instead, he asked for silence before saying a prayer. One of the absolutes in Jimmy's life was his tremendous faith. His feet were always planted firmly on the ground because he was rooted so deeply in his faith.

I had attended church with the Russells and knew how active and devoted they were to the administration of the church. They knew most of the parishioners—especially the young people—by their first names.

One of his closest confidants was Reverend Bobby Lawrence, his pastor at Clearview Baptist Church, which was located a block from his home. Jimmy had invited him, but he had another engagement and couldn't attend.

"I asked you all to join us tonight to share your honest opinions about me possibly running for the nomination for governor," Jimmy said. "Don't all speak at once."

Horace said, "Let's give it a shot. Why not?"

"It's a once-in-a-lifetime opportunity," said Carey.

Mrs. Russell said, "I think it's a wonderful opportunity, but we've got to consider the obstacles. What about the incredible demands for funding, the necessity for increased security, and the management of the campaign?"

"Yeah, Russ," said Milton. "You're going to be exposed to some pretty dangerous places during the campaign."

Sarah shouted, "Obama has survived—so far."

Milton said, "Yeah, but he's got the Secret Service."

Jimmy raised his hands and asked for calm. "I'll have protection."

Horace nudged Milton and whispered, "He's talking about the Lord, but he needs some big, bad men surrounding him."

Jimmy said, "I discussed the need for a top-notch security detail with Poindexter. He's been in touch with several law enforcement people already and assured me that ample protection would be a priority."

"What about the money?" asked Horace.

"Poindexter named several powerful Democrats in Alabama—and in other states—who want to target some of the southern GOP governors," Jimmy said. "These men think the GOP has ruled for much too long in these so-called red states. A group headed by Cleo Jones will begin a statewide drive to raise money as soon as I say yes to running."

Jones had made a fortune flipping houses and buildings in Birmingham and Huntsville. He loved the political arena and was widely known for saying, "Politics gets my blood boiling."

"Why you, Jimmy?" asked Milton. "No disrespect meant, but Poindexter has his pick of anyone in the state to back in this campaign."

"Wait a minute," Laci fired back. "I don't see how he can do any better than Daddy."

"Milt, I asked him the same thing," Jimmy said. "Poindexter cited my record, experience, and credentials. He thinks my family and my life story are big pluses."

"Daddy, do you really want to do this?" Laci asked.

Jimmy looked into Laci's eyes and said, "Baby, I'm leaning that way."

"If it's what you want, I'm all in," Laci said. "And don't worry about the ads and websites. I've got that covered."

"What about a campaign manager?" Lady Di asked.

"Steven Poindexter has volunteered to manage the campaign," Jimmy replied. "He has the experience and the contacts."

The whole assembly said, "Wow!" They understood the impact Poindexter's name could have for Jimmy's campaign.

Clifton asked, "What do you want me to do if you decide to seek the nomination?"

It went back and forth for at least two hours.

Finally, in a controlled voice, Jimmy said, "I have decided to run." He asked everyone to hold hands and asked his son-in-law to pray.

Malcolm was a deacon and Sunday school superintendent at Clearview Baptist. The main theme in his prayer was asking God for protection and guidance during the campaign.

Laci had tears in her eyes, and her mom consoled her. Laci was happy for her father, but she was also concerned for his safety.

Pete, his 12 year old grandson, yelled, "Git um, Granddaddy!"

Chapter 2

Who is James Earl Russell?

Jimmy had to notify the powers that be that he had decided to run, and we had to get out of his way. Jimmy had to touch base with two of the men who would play a major role in the campaign.

"Brother Jones, how are you?" Jimmy said. "Listen, I've decided to run and would appreciate any help you can offer,"

Cleo exclaimed, "Fantastic! There's no time to loose! Jimmy, I'll do everything in my power to help you win. We'll clean out that den of vipers in Montgomery."

"Maybe we can get together tomorrow to talk," said Jimmy.

"Fine! Have you talked to Poindexter tonight?" asked Jones.

"No, I called you first. I'm getting ready to call him now."

Jimmy called Poindexter and said, "Steven, I've decided to give it a shot. I'm going to give it all I've got."

"Great! I kind of thought you would, Jimmy. I've already contacted two men who can really help us."

"Who are they?" asked Jimmy.

"Robert Murphy is a wealthy businessman and a neighbor of mine. Dr. Chad Humphreys is an influential power broker in north Alabama. Humphreys is driving over from Scottsboro in the morning, and we'll get things rolling. These men know how to energize the base and get them to open their wallets at the same time," said a confident Poindexter.

"Steven, I don't know how to thank you for all of this. But, man, I appreciate it."

"Listen, I think you have a lot better chance of winning this *whole thing* than you think, Jimmy."

He worried about his diction all the time. That was one reason he had such trouble meeting girls when he first arrived at State. He knew absolutely nothing about public speaking. He had never been asked to stand in front of a group of people and speak. Jimmy was terrified at the thought of having to stand in front of a group of people and talk.

One of the classes he dreaded most was a public speaking class taught by a 'Bama State legend. Dr. Roland Greenlea demanded a lot of his students. You couldn't simply impress your classmates with your speaking ability in the classroom and get an A. No, Dr. Greenlea had some much more challenging plans for his pupils.

Each student had to develop a strong speech with a message that other students would be interested in hearing. Then you had to actually go out on campus to a very public hangout, get their attention, and make your pitch.

When Jimmy realized that this assignment constituted 33 percent of his semester grade, he almost passed out from fright. He was also very insecure. Jimmy had to find a topic that would grab and hold the attention of students on campus.

A lot of folks were talking about the riots that were going on during the sixties, and he thought that might be a good topic. He had to research the topic just like Greenlea had told them to do. He called a cousin who lived in Detroit during the riots to get firsthand accounts. He read everything he could find on the subject. He got in front of the mirror in his dorm room and practiced. He asked teammates to listen to the speech in the lobby of the dorm. He didn't know it at the time, but that assignment did wonders for his self-esteem.

On the day of his speech, Jimmy was confident that he could do it. To make a long story short, Jimmy started out kind of shaky, but he got stronger as he talked to the students in front of the cafeteria.

As he scanned the crowd—the way Greenlea taught him to do it—he saw the instructor in the back of the crowd. Greenlea had a clipboard in his hand and seemed to enjoy Jimmy's speech.

That was the first time in his life that he realized the awesome power of communication. Jimmy knew his subject matter, and the audience appreciated it. Jimmy got an A on the speech, but he earned so much more. I was in that crowd, and I had to make sure they applauded the right way … you know?

By his junior year, Jimmy was on the dean's list every semester. Fraternities came calling, and Jimmy finally decided to pledge Kappa Alpha Psi with me. During pledge season, he met the woman who would change his life. She was the woman Jimmy had always visualized.

Diane Lauren Nelson was a freshman from Birmingham. She was majoring in English with a minor in political science and worked in the library.

She had received a partial academic scholarship and used the work-study program to cover the balance of her fees. She was eager, smart, and a tireless worker. Diane was a petite woman with hazel-brown eyes and a figure to die for. Ms. Nelson was nobody's fool. She placed her work ahead of everything. The guys who tried to hit on her knew they had better come "correct."

Her dad, Calvin, worked at US Steel as a laborer, and her mom, Mattie, was a practical nurse at St. Vincent's Hospital.

These were people I had known for most of my life. She had two siblings, including an older brother, Timothy, who I knew very well. Tim was killed during an ambush by the Viet Cong near An Khe in 1969. Diane has a younger sister named Marsha.

Tim's death really grieved the girls, especially during the time they were making plans for the future. Diane and Marsha took a long time to cope with the loss. The loss tore me up too. Every time any special occasion came around, the pain of the loss would be amplified.

Diane and Marsha were made of some pretty tough stuff, and moving forward was all they knew. Nothing was going to stop them from accomplishing their goals ... nothing.

On a muggy evening in August of 1971, a chance meeting between Diane and Jimmy took place. Jimmy was about to open the door to the student recreation center when a cute, little girl was about to go inside.

As the gentleman he was, Jimmy opened the door for her. She thanked him, and Jimmy has been hopelessly smitten ever since. He was taken by her from day one. All he talked about that night was the beautiful girl he opened the door for.

He couldn't concentrate on the card game or shooting pool. He just had to say something to her or not sleep that night. He decided to gather intelligence about her. What's her name? Does she have a boyfriend? What dorm does she live in?

She was relatively new on campus, and he didn't get much information besides her dorm and where she worked. Jimmy had to get up the courage to actually ask her some of these questions.

Diane was drinking a soda and talking to a friend at one of the tables. Jimmy walked over with the typical swagger of a popular gridiron star and asked if he could he sit with them. Both girls said alright. Jimmy had trouble formulating coherent sentences that night. The girls looked at each other and grinned.

Finally, Jimmy reclined in his chair, took a deep breath, and said, "I came over here to ask you your name."

She smiled and said, "I'm Diane Nelson ... and your name is?"

"My name is Jimmy Russell, and I'm a junior here."

Diane's friend excused herself, and the two stayed at the table until the rec center closed. After walking her to the dorm, Jimmy went to his dorm in complete bedazzlement. He was in love.

Jimmy said, "When I touch her, my heart races. I want her so badly that it actually hurts. I love the way she eats her food, the way she laughs, the way she walks, the curves in her lips, the way she smells, and the beauty of her skin. When she talks, I am mesmerized."

It sounded like love to me. Their union has been solid since then, and many people believe it has grown stronger. They have always looked to each other for support—for whatever is needed. Their bond is amazing.

The two were an item on campus. Most of their spare time was spent in each other's company. Not much for parties and social events, they preferred quiet time in the dorm lobby or talking on the steps of the library.

They loved going downtown to the movies or attending church on Dexter Avenue. Jimmy loved to gaze into Diane's eyes. Diane's friends knew she was just as taken with him as he was with her. This was no one-way street by any stretch. It was almost understood that they would eventually marry, but nobody knew when.

During Jimmy's senior year, that question was finally answered. Two weeks before his graduation, Russ asked me to serve as a witness. Jimmy graduated in August, and they planned to live with her parents for the time being.

By the time they married, Jimmy was already a part of the family. When the two went home for holidays, Jimmy spent quite a bit of time at the Nelson home instead of traveling to Whitney. Mr. Nelson loved him like the son he had lost.

The Nelsons never missed a home football game at 'Bama State. Everyone thought that Jimmy would give pro football a shot. He had other plans. No one really knew the terrible pain he suffered in his right knee from tendinitis or the left shoulder that ached from time to time.

He had fractured two fingers in his junior year and continued to play. Russell only weighed a little over two hundred pounds. He could just imagine the type of pounding he would take in the pros. Even before the end of his senior season, they decided that his football playing days were over.

He was promised a coaching position at a Birmingham high school before he graduated. To supplement his salary as a teacher and the small coaching supplement, he planned to teach summer school.

Jimmy's parents, two sisters, and a brother drove over from Whitney, and Diane's parents and her sister came down from Birmingham for Jimmy's graduation. The graduation ceremony was in the football stadium. It was an oppressively hot day and we prayed for a brief ceremony. He never thought he would actually graduate from college. I was happy and proud of him because I knew how far he had come. By that time, we were really like blood brothers.

I respect Jimmy Russell—probably more than any man I know. He is a solid, honest human being. There is no one more loyal than Russ. If you're his friend, he'll go all the way with you. For him, it's God, family, and friends—in that order.

After he got the teaching position, he sent Diane money for beauty salon visits, washing clothes, or just having money in her pockets. Jimmy took over for her parents. He even worked at a department store for extra money during the Christmas holidays. He saved religiously because he knew they needed a place of their own.

In the meantime, he enjoyed his stay with the Nelsons. The Nelson home was a two-story frame house with a finished basement. The basement had its own bathroom, and it served as Jimmy's "apartment."

Diane would come home on weekends, and the couple attended church with her parents. Church was something that was nonnegotiable for the Russell family. Both of them had grown up in the church. Their lives had been inundated with scriptures, gospel music, and Baptist preaching. They wouldn't have it any other way.

Diane's dad was a deacon in their church—just like Jimmy's dad. Religion is one thing, but real, unbridled faith is quite another. The newlyweds were true believers.

Faith in God was an absolute must in their marriage. It was all coming together, and Russ and his new bride were a happy couple. In life, there are always ups and downs. And, one of those downs was right around the corner.

In December 1973, Daddy Nelson was diagnosed with advanced prostate cancer. His last examination had been in the fall of 1971. Mrs. Mattie had been on him about going to the doctor, but like many men of his generation, in the African-American community, he continuously put it off.

Even with this dire prognosis, the family was optimistic about his chances of survival. A prostatectomy was scheduled for December 12, and after a brief recovery from the surgery, radiation would commence. After additional scans were performed, the doctor informed the family that some of the cancer had escaped the prostate; chemotherapy would be necessary.

Calvin Nelson was a proud man who never needed anyone to lean on, but this was different. He began to sit alone a lot and not join in conversations. Mattie was really worried about depression setting in—and her husband losing the will to fight. She encouraged Jimmy to talk to him as much as possible and get him out of the house. Jimmy asked him to go shopping with him for Christmas gifts, but Cal said no.

When Jimmy asked again, Cal changed his mind. They visited three stores and ate lunch on the way home. Cal actually enjoyed the outing very much.

Chemotherapy was to begin the following Monday, and Cal understood that he might not have the strength to do some of the things he liked to do after that. When he thought about the treatments, a terrible gloom overtook him.

As strong as he was, this thing was a test for every fiber of his being. He had hardly ever missed a day of work, but the mention of cancer completely devastated him. He had seen an uncle die from throat cancer and an aunt die from colon cancer after languishing in pain for months.

Diane would come home and spend most of the weekend with her dad, watching television and praying with him. During the Christmas holidays that year, the Nelson household was not as lively or celebratory as usual. Cal would have good days after chemo and bad days too. He had terrible bouts of vomiting, and his weight dropped by twenty pounds.

After another scan was performed, the doctor informed him that the cancer had spread. Cal began to accept his fate. He wanted to tell the entire family what the doctor had told him and Jimmy that morning. He asked the family to join him in the den that afternoon.

They were all extremely quiet, and Mrs. Mattie finally just broke down and sobbed uncontrollably. Diane and Marsha cried and embraced their dad. Cal's younger brother, Curtis, was there, and tears streamed from his eyes. Jimmy took Mattie out of the room and consoled her as best he could. It was a Christmas they would never forget.

I have known the family since I was in elementary school, and I had to be there for support. Mr. Nelson had always been nice to me, and I grew up with Tim.

In February, Cal took a turn for the worst and was rushed to the emergency room. His temperature was very high, and he experienced some rectal bleeding. The doctors ran tests and determined that he should be home with his family. He was assigned hospice care, and on the morning of February 28, the hospice attendant told Mattie she didn't think he would live through the day.

The family members took turns at his bedside and kept a constant, prayerful vigil. At 3:10 that afternoon, Marsha heard her father gasp. When she couldn't find his pulse, she screamed for Mattie to come in the room. The hospice attendant and everyone else ran in to check on Cal.

Mrs. Mattie frantically listened for any breathing and checked for a pulse, but she knew he was gone. The attendant looked in each person's eyes to confirm what Mattie already knew. Just five years earlier, Timothy's death had taken a grim toll on the family. Now, they had to summon the strength to deal with more pain and grief. At just sixty years of age, Cal was gone.

At the somber funeral, Mama Mattie cried until she was completely exhausted. The children started to worry about her health. Jimmy's father and mother had made the trip up to Birmingham for the funeral. They both liked Calvin Nelson very much. The Nelsons had visited them in the country several times, and the families had grown close. Pastor Lawrence preached the eulogy and was visibly hurt by the loss of one of his staunchest supporters at the church.

Nelson had been a strong chairman of the deacon board and a faithful friend of the pastor. Jimmy knew that he would have to fill the void left by such a powerful man, and he was intent on doing it. After the burial and gathering at the Nelson home, Jimmy sat at the kitchen table with Mattie while the girls showed people out.

Jimmy wanted to assure Mattie that he was there to support her. Whatever she needed, he would do everything in his power to supply it. Mattie was deeply moved and wept in total gratitude. Her husband had left her in decent shape financially. The mortgage on the home had been satisfied for some time, and there were no large debts. She made one request right away. She wanted Jimmy and Diane to stay with her until they had saved enough for a down payment on a house. She had overheard them discussing renting an apartment in the near future. Jimmy and Diane talked it over and decided to remain in the house until they saved the necessary funds.

When Diane needed to get back to school, they packed her luggage into Jimmy's 1967 Chevy. The car was seldom dirty and always protected with coat of the best wax. The interior was immaculate. He hated when people got in his car with muddy shoes. Aside from Diane, Jimmy's true love was that blue Chevy with the spotless chrome wheels. Russ said the trip back to Montgomery was tough.

The trip to Montgomery usually took about an hour and forty-five minutes, but it seemed longer that night. Diane was pensive and gazed out the window quite a bit. I tried to cheer her up, but thought it might be best to back off a little. She needed her space. When we were entering Prattville, Alabama, Diane said, "It hurt me so much to see my daddy suffer like that."

"I know how you felt about your father, and your pain is my pain," I said. "I loved him too."

We pulled off the interstate and held each other. We had to pick up the pieces. Tragedy had struck, but there was work to be done. We both knew that dealing with the pain of losing Papa Nelson so close to the loss of her brother would be an immense challenge. Our faith helped us get through it.

Chapter 3

A Time to Weep and a Time to Laugh

Mrs. Morris told me about an event that took place during spring break in 1974. She chatted with Diane after a church service at Clearview. Mrs. Morris recalled the talk as if it happened yesterday.

***

"Sister Sarah, I can visualize my father standing in the kitchen," Diane said. "He is reciting scripture to Mama, in a playful way, and invariably Ecclesiastes would emerge. That man loved those scriptures. If things weren't going real well, he would start quoting Ecclesiastes 3:4."

"That's the one that talks about a time to weep and a time to laugh, right?" Sarah asked.

"Yes, but it continues with a time mourn and a time to dance. For some strange reason, it got me thinking about my terrible bouts with this awful grief. I had to take account of where I was in my life. I was looking out my dorm window. To make things worse, it was raining. As the gloom and despair began to take over, a wonderful thing happened. I began to think about my blessings. I have a wonderful, loving husband, a devoted mother, and a fantastic sister. 'Bama State has been good for me too. I started to realize that I had no right to be sad. It was time for me to laugh and dance instead of focusing on the unhappy moments in my life."

"Amen!" Sarah said and she hugged Diane.

***

"She's such a sweet girl—and it was really good to see her perk up," Mrs. Morris said.

"Looking at her now, you wouldn't think that a woman as strong as she is would let anything get her down," I said.

"My boy, you just keep living. A lot can happen to test your very soul. I know how hard she worked in school. She was always worried about Jimmy having to shoulder all the financial obligations alone."

"I want to know what happened later that year," I said jokingly. "Who knows—I might write a book about the Russell family one day."

"Mrs. Morris told me I needed to talk to Diane's sister to get a firsthand account of what happened. Fortunately, Marsha Burroughs is often called on to participate in career days at schools in the area, and we met at one of them. I asked if I could talk to her for a moment. She agreed, and we sat at a table in the school's media center. Mrs. Burroughs started to reminisce about that eventful period in their lives.

***

Diane went to summer school every year so she could graduate early. Her target graduation date was August 1975. She stiffened her resolve; nothing was going to stop her.

Her goal was to finish as soon as possible in order to help Jimmy save for their home. There was renewed excitement and a defined purpose in her life. Her letters to Jimmy let him know that she was on the mend.

Her melancholy moods were replaced by an upbeat, happy spirit. This made Jimmy, mom, and me very happy, and we looked forward to her graduation. Her graduation turned out to be a real family affair.

Jimmy, mom, Uncle Curtis, and I drove onto State's campus that extremely humid August morning. Jimmy's parents and all of his siblings attended too. It was time for Diane to reap the rewards of a job well done.

Diane was the salutatorian of her class, just missing valedictorian by a tenth of a point. Diane introduced all of us to the librarian (today's media specialist) she had worked under for three years. We walked over to Wills Hall to meet her favorite English professor, Dr. Radford Ellis. We stopped at a bench near the cafeteria in a nice shaded area. Mama needed a break from the constant walking, and so did some other folks.

Diane wanted the family to eat lunch with her in the rec center. They had nice salads and sandwiches and it was cool inside. Uncle Curtis really liked the way they prepared his Reuben sandwich.

The graduation ceremony started at 5:00 and was over at 6:45. Diane had to stay over that night, and Jimmy would have to come back for her in a friend's van to pack up her belongings.

We were extremely proud of what she had accomplished. We were thrilled that she was coming home. Mama would have her daughter there full-time, at least for a while. Jimmy would have his beloved wife there, and I would have my best friend back home.

Weekends were good, but not enough time for Jimmy. He got up bright and early that Saturday morning to go back to Montgomery to get his wife.

Diane had appointments with two principals the following Tuesday. She had sent out resumes to ten schools in Jefferson County. There were several openings for English teachers in the Birmingham City System and the Jefferson County School System. With the excellent grades on her transcript, she didn't have too much concern about getting a job. A good English teacher is a real find for a principal. She was a teacher who actually loved teaching grammar, if you can believe that!

Her last interview proved to be the decisive one. She was offered two jobs that day, but Amherst High was the one she chose. The school, which was located in the eastern part of the county, was a forty-minute drive from Mama's house.

But she needed car. She had taken the Greyhound Bus home for weekend visits and hadn't thought that much about a car. Jimmy thought that a small car, like a Volkswagen, would probably be best.

They finally settled on a 1970 Chevy Nova. Diane complained that the car had no air-conditioning, which many did not at the time, and just an AM radio. Jimmy said, "Crawl before you can walk." Every time she complained, he would say the word *house* three or four times.

Back then, most school systems began the school year shortly after Labor Day. These days, most schools start the second week of August. Diane's first teaching assignment was just two weeks away. She was really excited and already writing lesson plans. A stickler for organization, she lost no time detailing how each class period would be divided into segments.

Some of the ideas were borrowed from things Jimmy had told her about how football practice time was divided into segments to make sure the boys didn't goof off. He said they went from one drill to another, seamlessly. His kids knew what to expect every day in practice. This type of regimen always helped with their focus during games. Diane seized upon some of these ideas and knew she could make it work in her classes.

Once the school year began, Diane was all business. Her paperwork was always on time, and the discipline in her classes was excellent. Her kids respected her, and the school administration thought they had found a real gem. Better yet, she loved her job. The idea of actually helping a child learn and grow was fulfilling. To see the light come on in a child's eyes brought tremendous satisfaction to her.

She had found her life's work. She understood that she would never get rich doing the job, but she loved getting up and going to work. Our mom always said that liking what you do is very important. Teaching is what she had always wanted to do. She had the opportunity to have an effect on young lives. To this end, she was very serious.

Diane wanted to be a true professional in her work. She studied different techniques in classroom management and searched for the best workshops and in-service opportunities.

Never satisfied with the status quo, she knew there were better ways of doing things. It was the beginning of a wonderful career in education. She actively involved parents and guardians as much as possible. She wanted them to take ownership and responsibility in the formative years of their children's lives.

Her work kept her mind off the unpleasant thought about daddy's passing, for a time anyway. Sometimes sitting alone in her classroom during prep periods brought back the sickening feelings of loss. She realized that the gloom was just beneath the surface and more prayer was necessary. She decided to seek counseling from Pastor Lawrence.

The talks with Reverend Lawrence on Saturday mornings restored a sense of clarity for her. Dede(what I call my sis) started to understand that part of the problem was keeping too much anguish repressed. She needed to talk about it more.

She made it a point to open up more to Mama and Jimmy. Dede also reached out to me. We had always been close, lifelong best friends. My life was also changing, and I needed advice from my big sister.

The laughter had returned to Diane's life—in a big way. Spending more time with me and relying more on the church had done wonders for her. More challenges were certainly coming, but finding the proper support was the answer.

She had help all around her, but she hadn't taken advantage of it before. Dede was on her way to becoming an emotionally healthy person who could help others. She stopped trying to do everything on her own.

It was a time of discovery for the young couple. Jimmy was trying to make a reputation as a good teacher and coach. Diane was trying to realize her dreams of becoming a good teacher.

Both of them wanted to be active in their church and community. Jimmy realized he had a lot to offer to the youth in the community through the YMCA. Diane taught a Sunday school class for teens and led a youth choir at church. They were gifted young people, but they were just scratching the surface in the seventies. The Russells were on their way to being community leaders and much more.

Horace mentioned that he was enrolled in night classes at law school. Jimmy had always been interested in the law, but he thought it was an unattainable fantasy. Hey, my brother-in-law is a pragmatist, he dismissed the thought and concentrated on buying a home.

Once Diane heard about the discussion, she was definitely interested. She immediately planted the seed in Jimmy's head that law school should be a goal for him. In the early eighties, after they bought a home, Jimmy enrolled in night classes at the law school.

Diane told him that she would ask for a teaching assignment in summer school to help with the fees. It took three and half years of night school and summer quarters for Jimmy to finish law school.

Then, there was the monster they call the Alabama Bar Examination. There were tales of people failing the test multiple times, but Jimmy had faith he could pass it on the first attempt.

He would have to prepare and prepare hard for the exam. The exam was only administered at the end of February and the end of July. Jimmy wanted to shoot for the February test date, and he had to file by October. There were filing fees and application fees. There was also a $475 initial testing fee. He thought about the folks who had to repeat this torture and pay even higher fees for successive attempts.

It was a grueling two-day examination with two hundred questions and plenty of essay questions involving civil procedure, real property, trusts, future interest, constitutional law, and other subjects. Jimmy immersed himself in the material. It would take nights and full weekends of sheer concentration to pass the test the first time. Diane and I took turns asking questions and reviewing materials with Jimmy. Mama jokingly said she would pray for him.

He knew he would have to amass at least 256 points out of a possible 400 points to pass. It was right in the middle of football season, and Jimmy was really strung out.

He had spent quite a bit on bar review study guides, and the money was running out. Early on, he decided not to enroll in one of the bar review classes that cost between $350 to $400.

Money had gotten pretty tight in the Russell home. With the mortgage, utilities, groceries, Diane's car note (she had moved up to a 1979 Buick, with air), furniture bills, clothing bills, and miscellaneous expenses, the budget was stretched to the limit. Then, Dear Mama came to the rescue.

Hey, mama knew they were struggling, but she didn't want to meddle. Mama had always been very frugal, and she was able to talk the "kids" into accepting a loan. With this loan, a lot of pressure was lifted off the couple so they could concentrate on Jimmy passing the test.

After months of focused study, the big day was here. Jimmy secured a substitute for the two days of testing. He was anxious to tackle the test and get it over with. On the way to the test site, he said words like *torts*, *evidence*, and *family law* were buzzing around his brain. *"Boy, let me put some of this stuff down on paper before I forget it," he kept repeating to himself.*

In the test room, he felt pretty confident. He took deep breaths, sat back in his seat, and focused on each question.

After two tense days of testing, Jimmy could finally get in his pickup and go home. He would know the results in May. Until then, he would pray for the best.

When he got home that evening, Diane said, "Well?"

"I think I did all right," Jimmy said. "That stuff was really drilled into me." *Could this be a time to laugh and dance?*

Chapter 4

The Proof is in the Deed

In the northwestern part of the state, another family was steeped in aspirations too. Their goals might have been slightly contrary to those of the Russells, but they were just as earnest. *Blood in, Blood Out* by Bob Thornton Ross—a sad story of hatred, violence, and revenge—is about the infamous Guthrie clan.

Percy and Sheldon Guthrie of rural Lamar County, three miles from the Mississippi state line, were very determined folks. Their home was a haven for some of the most dangerous felons in Alabama. The Guthrie brothers were out to make a name for themselves. Percy, the older of the brothers, was aspiring to be one of the most fearsome white nationalists in the south. Sheldon hung on his every word.

Percy had just finished a stretch in the state prison at Atmore for armed robbery. That only gave him street cred with the people in his circle. Percy was six foot two and weighed about 170 pounds, but he could handle himself in a scrap. Not many people tried the man from Raven's Trace in spite of his lean, wiry frame.

Sheldon was a big man. At six foot four and 250 pounds, the amateur boxer was the muscle of the family. Not wanting to exercise his brain unduly, he looked to his older brother to make all the plans.

Percy was just plain mean. His green eyes were saddened by years of bitterness and strife. The bearded man was also very intelligent and would be a handful for law enforcement.

The nationalist movement had taken root in New Zealand, Australia, Germany, Paraguay, Canada, and the United States. Percy was a recruiter in his neck of the woods, and his little brother was one of his main targets. Their double-wide mobile home, situated at the end of a dirt road, was located in Raven's Trace in southwestern Lamar County. The Guthrie trailer had become a hangout for some of the roughest customers in northwest Alabama. Here, you could brag about your latest assault on a Jew or a black person and win praise from everyone. By the way, the movement had no love for gays or lesbians either.

Most of these well-armed visitors were affiliated with one or more of the hate groups identified by the Southern Poverty Law Center in Montgomery, Alabama. Weapons of every type were being stockpiled as if total war was at hand. These hate-filled meetings could only produce one result: violence. Percy was always the center of attention. He railed against just about everything. He despised the government, hated "Catholics, Jews, and niggers," and couldn't stand policemen.

New converts were tasked with proving their loyalty to the cause of white power. Percy saw to it that no one just walked into this fraternity. Targets were identified, and new converts had to carry out the planned assaults. Sometimes the result was death. Percy had five notches on the handle of his .357 Magnum, and he wanted more. Once a convert completed his assignment, he would be welcomed into the "bond."

The Guthrie clan was known for trouble with the law. From their uncle being busted for his whiskey stills to an aunt who was busted for selling meth, the Guthrie clan had no love for the law.

The Guthrie patriarch was a well-known gambler and car thief. Their dad was also known for his quick, fiery temper. A hard man, Pop Guthrie preferred using a razor instead of a gun on an enemy.

They had a cousin killed in a gunfight over a fifty-dollar loan. Violence was something they understood. It was not the last resort for the Guthries; it was usually the preliminary action to solve a problem.

"Blood in and blood out" was the family motto. To get into the clan, you had to be willing to spill some blood. Once in the gang, the only way to get out was to die. There was no reasoning with them. You deal their way or get out of the way. To add fuel to an already smoldering tempest, most of these guys were drug abusers.

Percy absolutely loved corn liquor and kept a gallon jug in the trailer at all times. Sheldon preferred marijuana and a lot of beer. There were usually bottles of Jim Beam or Wild Turkey on the coffee table, and country music played at all their meetings. These meetings could go on for hours—and sometimes until morning. Percy called the shots in the end. It was his call when the set was over, it was his call when they would get together again, and it was his call when the next victim would incur their fury.

A new convert, Wallace Duncan—a high school dropout—was up for an assignment in Riverside, a small town just off highway 107 in Fayette County. Fayette County was located east of Lamar, and Wallace knew the area well. The target was what Percy called an "uppity nigger" who needed a lesson in how to talk to white people. The man Percy spoke of was Samuel Laster, a bank teller who asked a man not to cut in line in the bank. The man ignored Laster, and the guard told the man to leave. Unfortunately, the stubborn man at the bank was one of Percy's disciples. Duncan's job was to beat Laster with an aluminum bat so he would never forget his place again.

To make sure the job got done, a veteran of the nationalist movement rode along with Wallace. The men scouted Laster's movements for two days before deciding when and where to strike. They knew that Laster drove by the school to pick up his daughter after her basketball practice. They drove to the school gym at dusk and waited in the parking lot for Laster's daughter to come out. Laster described the events of that day in an interview with a local radio station.

***

When Kim, my daughter, was about to get in the car, a man shouted out that I had a flat on the rear passenger side. I immediately got out to check the tire, but before I could even bend over to check the tire … out of the corner of my eye, I saw this man raising something over my head. Kim screamed, and I threw my arm up to block the object he was swinging at me.

Well, I felt a terrible pain in my forearm, and I covered my head as best I could because he kept striking me with what I finally realized was a bat. My side was aching, and my shoulder was also struck. When I turned away from him, I caught a blow on my jaw that basically knocked me out. Kim told me that other parents were yelling and calling the police and paramedics. Kim thought he was going to kill me. I did too.

While Duncan was standing over me, bitter, hateful rants were spewing from his mouth. He said, "Nigger, you'll know the next time how to talk a white man. This will teach your black ass how to respect a white man." By that time, I was semi-conscious and will never forget the hostility in his voice. Kim said that she and two of the parents were trying to stop the bleeding from my nose and mouth.

The nearest hospital was twenty-two miles away, and the sheriff's department had jurisdiction in that tiny hamlet. Duncan and his cohort were long gone by the time they responded. Fortunately, two of the people in the parking lot wrote down the tag number of the assailant's Dodge Charger.

Six months later, Duncan was arrested outside Meridian, Mississippi, after a car chase through two counties. He confessed—proudly—to the deed. Two months later, his cohort and accomplice of that night, Frank Bly, was arrested in Monroe, Louisiana. He too confessed and wore his nationalist brand with pride.

I will move my family to Michigan after I recover and I don't think I'll ever travel south again.

***

Ross went on to say that the "assignments" continued and various parts of the state were targeted. More members were recruited, and the hatred spread like a malignancy.

Jimmy thought racism was the absolute scourge in our land. He saw it as "a pestilence, a disease, and a monster with an unquenchable thirst for destruction."

These scary images are not so overstated in the black community. The amount of damage racism can exact on a person over a lifetime is incalculable. Jimmy said, "It takes an extremely strong man to resist the arrows of hatred in such volume."

Being the subject of constant, unadulterated discrimination takes a toll. Weaker folks don't survive it. They give up trying to fit into a society that they've been told, for so long, belongs to someone else. The ugly stain of second-class citizenship has deeply scarred so many for far too long. Mr. Ross said the Guthrie faction had little sympathy for the people they decided to hate.

Well, the Guthries and their friends would do their best to widen the gap between whites and blacks. They had no sympathy for Jews, Catholics, blacks, or government officials. Time for discussions and "peace in our time" was empty rhetoric to them. They were an angry, aggressive group of people who wanted to punish the world because of their plight.

Percy always said, "If we make them bleed enough, they'll get the message sooner or later."

To them, violence worked—and you'd get everybody's attention if it focused in the right direction. Woe to the poor, unsuspecting person who made Percy's list.

***

In hot, humid Birmingham, James Russell focuses on something entirely different. While he sits in his downtown law office, he thinks back to those lean, exciting days in the early eighties.

conversation, and Mr. Jones added a sentence here and there. It was Poindexter's show. He had the facts, which broke down each candidate's strong points and weak points, prepared by his team in Huntsville.

Poindexter asked Jones for opinions on two of the people seeking the nomination. Jones had done business with one of them and knew the other through an associate. The meeting could not have been more important. To Jimmy, it had cleared the field of a lot of the unknowns.

The next day, Cleo called Jimmy and said, "That damn boy knows his stuff." Jimmy could not have agreed more.

Poindexter had already lined up three engagements for Jimmy in north Alabama. He would be flown to Huntsville, and his first speech would be delivered to the Kiwanis Club.

Jimmy's years in the courtroom helped tremendously with his age-old fear of public speaking, but this was an entirely different arena. The pressure was intense, and he had to be at his best. He would have to imagine his audience as a jury of men and women he tried to sway. The old inhibitions about his background, the poverty, and the lack of social grooming as a youth had to be moved to the deepest recesses of his mind. In place of those emotional restraints, he would have to show confidence, resolve, and empathy for everyday Alabamians. Jimmy talked to himself before every engagement and he was starting to believe what he was preaching.

After flying to Huntsville, they would take a car to Athens. Jimmy would speak to the Limestone Democrats the following morning.

His last engagement was in Scottsboro with the Jackson County Kiwanis Club. Poindexter wanted to get some immediate exposure for Jimmy in a part of the state he was not well known. Poindexter made sure all the major newspapers would cover the events. The plan was for Jimmy to introduce himself and lay out his general stance on the hot-button issues of the day.

During the two-day swing through north Alabama, Jimmy stayed in touch with Diane. She was his anchor. He always felt a sense of comfort when he talked to her.

She told him that Cleo Jones was stumping for cash all over the metropolitan area. Any Democrat worth his salt was asked to fork out to support their native son. Diane also told him that Marsha had finished building the websites.

My room was always adjacent to Mr. Russell's when we stayed at a hotel. The security team had rooms on our floor also. In the early days of the campaign, there were only three men assigned to the protection detail and occasionally local law enforcement would lend support.

Jimmy had a speaking engagement at Westbury Baptist Church on the following Sunday during the afternoon service. Since there were strict limits on the amount of time allotted for Jimmy's speech, they had to condense the speech. They covered the important issues. Diane kept Jimmy informed the way she had always done. Two days away from his love seemed like a month.

Coverage of Jimmy's north Alabama run was very positive. Terms like *confident, assertive, direct,* and *relaxed* were used to describe Jimmy's delivery. The jury was still out on substance. They had to get to know him before making any assumptions about things like character. They felt like it was a good start for his first appearance in that arena. People were starting to talk about the man from Birmingham.

The plan was for Jimmy to stump hard in the Birmingham metro, which would serve as his base. First, he had to win over, as many voters as possible, in metro areas that were heavily GOP and had been that way for a generation or more. Suburban cities like Hoover, Vestavia, and Homewood would be tough places to gain a foothold. Sticking to the initial plan, he would still campaign in all of those places. They would not shy away from the tough challenges. Jimmy had to show them that he would be governor for everybody.

When we got back to Birmingham on Saturday, he immediately started preparing for his speech. He practiced in front of Mrs. Russell and me until he felt he had it down perfectly.

As Jimmy and Diane pulled into the east parking lot at Westbury, they saw Marsha, Malcolm, and Pete getting out of their car. Inside the church, they saw Carey and his wife Gloria. Sitting next to Carey and his family was the Crittenden family. I had a front pew seat next to Mrs. Russell. I did not want to miss anything.

When Reverend Talley summoned Jimmy to the pulpit, Cleo Jones and his wife walked in. In the rear of the church, Jimmy spotted the well-known news anchor, Robert Sorenson, and his cameraman.

Horace entered in a huff and sat in the center of the huge church. Craig was six foot three and weighed nearly 260 pounds. He always bragged about his full head of hair and joked about Jimmy's receding hairline. Jimmy wondered where Craig's wife was that evening. Later, he found out that Craig's wife, Priscilla, was a featured speaker at her own church that evening. Cliff, Sylvia, and their two children were already there. Even eighty-five-year-old Uncle Curtis was in attendance that night.

Jimmy took his place behind the podium. He looked polished, and his suit fit very well. He had polished his shoes and gotten a haircut the day before. Jimmy had gained a few pounds since his 'Bama State days. He weighed about 235 pounds, but he was in pretty good shape because of his frequent walks at the track.

His glasses gave him a look of distinction and intelligence. Jimmy had good posture, and his voice resonated through the large edifice.

Mrs. Russell remarked later that Jimmy seemed to enjoy the stage like never before.

Jimmy followed the previous script with one obvious exception. Instead of merely introducing himself, he introduced his entire family. He also asked his friends and their families to stand. He was a lot more cordial in this presentation than in the north Alabama circuit where he was all business.

He laid out his general stances on the issues and formally introduced himself as a candidate for Alabama's highest office. After a meet and greet with refreshments in the fellowship hall of the church, Jimmy and Diane went home to relax and reflect.

The next day, a small article in the newspaper discussed the candidacy of a local lawyer, James E. Russell, for the Democratic nomination for governor. It mentioned that his campaign was in high gear—and that Cleo Jones was a supporter. Jimmy would have preferred more details—especially about his ideas regarding taxes, public education, law and order, and gay marriage—but a little coverage was better than none at all. Jimmy had to get his name out there in a big way.

Poindexter was working with party leaders to organize a debate for the five candidates. They agreed to debate at the BJCC on October 4. Party representatives from all over the state set up the debate format. It was the only scheduled debate for the candidates, and it was a chance for the candidates to separate themselves from their rivals. The stage was set for a showdown in the Magic City.

Poindexter had briefed Russell about his competition. One of the stars was an African-American woman who was a defector from the GOP. Angela Watkins was a CPA at the firm Sutton & Croft. Poindexter had put an asterisk by her name to emphasize her potency. She was in her fifties, was a dynamite speaker, and wasn't hard to look at either. She was a divorcee with one son who was in college. A self-made woman who had worked her way up in a male-dominated profession, Watkins was at the top of her game. She couldn't be taken lightly. She had served in the state house and senate as a Republican. She was from Florence, a city in the northwestern part of the state.

Gordon Roberts was another candidate Poindexter thought was a handful too. Roberts was a wealthy dentist who had gotten into politics a decade before. He won a council seat to represent eastern Birmingham. After that, he ran and won a seat in the Alabama House of Representatives. Following that tenure, he won a seat on the Jefferson County Commission. He was also a dynamic speaker.

Another candidate was Justin Floyd, a professor at Seymour Tech in south Alabama. He had served on the Mobile City Council for two terms.

The final candidate was Marshall Curry, the owner of a flower shop in Enterprise. Curry had not been in politics before.

Poindexter said that these last two candidates were polling in the mid-to-low single digits and were not serious contenders.

Knowing the importance of the debate, Jimmy met with Cyrus Merrill, the head of the English department at Sheldon State University, to practice his delivery and review his notes.

Diane had written down some catchphrases she thought would be impactful. Merrill amended some of the phrases and added some of his own.

Merrill had been an advisor to many of the notable Democratic campaigns in the past fifteen years. Sheldon State had some of wealthiest alumni in Alabama. Merrill was an expert in the language arts. He taught public speaking for more than a decade and was an excellent speechwriter. Jimmy was in good hands for the two days of coaching by the master wordsmith.

As the debate drew near, Russell's camp was getting pretty anxious. The latest polling had Jimmy two points behind Watkins and four points behind Roberts. The debate would really help Jimmy if he delivered a knockout. We all knew it wouldn't be easy.

Chapter 6

It's Time to Shine

To fire the team up before a game at 'Bama State, head coach Leroy McAfee would get in the players' faces and shout, "It's time to shine, boys!" The players knew it was time to lay it all out there on the field. Jimmy knew it was time to put up or shut up. It was a proving ground, a test of will. For Jimmy, it was nothing new, but like he told Jones before the debate, "It's just another challenge—but, man, it's a big one!"

Merrill thought Jimmy had the material down, and he believed Jimmy would win the debate. The moderator was Dr. Meredith Lawson, a former professor and a published author. Lawson had moderated other debates and was a stickler for proper procedure. The party gave each candidate a list of general topics to be covered in the debate. A time limit was established for responses, and the questions were structured to reveal differences between the candidates.

The moderator's first round of questions focused on the state's immigration laws. Each candidate had to dive into this divisive issue, which Jimmy had rehearsed a hundred times. Watkins's response to the question was similar to Jimmy's, but her answer came off as cold and aloof.

Merrill had emphasized the need to frame each answer with an emotional appeal without looking phony. When Jimmy and Cleo met with Poindexter in Birmingham, they felt that one of Watkins's weaknesses might be the absence of emotion. She was all business, and they saw this as a vulnerability.

Roberts's answer was framed better, but the content was inconsistent during rebuttals. Another point Merrill drove home was the need for consistency. Poindexter's vetting team had noticed Roberts's lack of preparation. They thought he depended too much on his ability to charm.

Roberts was still very calm and got stronger in the next round of questions. Lawson started by asking Jimmy about his views on taxation. Jimmy's stance on fair taxation was nowhere near the views of Watkins or Floyd. Curry and Roberts didn't think the tax laws needed a complete overhaul. There was a spirited debate on this subject, and the moderator had to be quite forceful on occasion.

Other questions involved gun control, public education, charter schools, voting rights, and earmarks. The debate seemed to pit Watkins against Russell, which was all right with Jimmy. The more he could distance himself from her, the better. When it concluded, the Russell camp felt good about the results. Jimmy had been authoritative, confident, compassionate, and direct.

Some thought that he and Watkins tied, and others said that Roberts deserved more consideration. Either way, Jimmy was heard from that night. He was on a statewide stage, and he left it on the field. Coach Mac would have been proud.

Newspapers and social media seemed to think Jimmy Russell should be taken seriously. A newspaperman from Tuscumbia, in northwestern Alabama, used the word *equanimity* to describe Jimmy's demeanor under intense scrutiny.

Diane loved the term when she read the article. She said the journalist saw something in Jimmy that Alabamians should appreciate: the ability to remain calm when turmoil and chaos reigned. Some of the folks in Jimmy's circle had to look the word up, but Diane didn't. I've got to admit that I wasn't familiar with that one either.

People marveled that he didn't flinch in the face of pressure. A persistent theme in the chatter over the next few days was Jimmy's obvious prowess in thinking on his feet. Folks were labeling him as a man with backbone—something he would need even more in the days to come.

The major newspapers in Birmingham, Huntsville, Montgomery, Mobile, and Tuscaloosa wrote extensive pieces about the debate. In their articles, Jimmy was mentioned very prominently. He was being discussed across the state, which had been the goal of the campaign. Jimmy had to get his name out there, and now it was. The primary election was approaching, and the polls were tightening. There was only a single percentage point between Watkins, Roberts, and Russell. It was anybody's election.

Steven Poindexter would have none of it! The phone rang in Jimmy's office, and Poindexter exclaimed, "Jimmy, we have some stumping to do! There are a lot of votes in west Alabama for the taking."

Neither candidate had really worked that part of the state, with the exception of Roberts.

"Next we'll swing through the north again," Poindexter continued.

"Hey! I'm ready," Jimmy replied. "I'll ask Diane to go with me on this stump."

"That's a great idea. I'll bring Christy with me. It's time the ladies met anyway."

The next morning, the Cessna was waiting, and the hard-charging Democrats took off at ten o'clock for points west.

Diane and Christy talked as if they had known each other for years. Diane found out that Christy had met Steven at a book signing for Poindexter's first book. They had struck up a conversation at the reception following the signing—and the rest was history. Poindexter was just starting out in his quest to establish himself in the world of high finance.

Christy said, "I'm proud of Steve's accomplishments, Diane, but you've got some man yourself. I know you're just as proud of him,"

"God knows I am proud of Jimmy for being the man he is. We started with nothing, and he never whined. He just kept on working. He keeps his head down and continues to move forward—no matter what."

"Wow! The way you look at each other—it's like you're teenagers," Christy noted.

"Christy, I love Jimmy so much that being without him is inconceivable."

"Love does sustain through all kinds of trials, doesn't it?" Christy said.

The ladies bonded while carving out their own space in the sixteen-seat Cessna. They were separated from the men by choice.

I sat in the middle of the cabin. Man, that was one fine aircraft. I really enjoyed flying in the "Silver Lady."

After landing in Tuscaloosa, we drove to Eutaw, Livingston, and Butler. Poindexter had arranged for Jimmy's last speech that night in Tuscaloosa.

Jimmy spoke to the Democrats for Change, an organization that had formed three years earlier. The group included some disaffected Republicans who had grown weary of the absolute austere governance in Montgomery.

These new Democrats were still financially conservative—but not to the point of completely ignoring much-needed services in the state. The roads in Alabama were so bad that people were afraid to drive at night for fear of striking some of the monstrous potholes.

Republicans were intent on raiding the Education Trust Fund in order to placate constituents by not raising taxes. Even the incumbent Republican governor knew that a tax hike was a necessity. These new Dems were people who Jimmy needed to talk to in the worst way.

While Jimmy was speaking at the Hilton in Tuscaloosa that evening, a heckler interrupted him several times. Jimmy's security team moved toward the man, and he started to leave the room. Instead of leaving, the man lunged in the direction of the podium.

Tyrone Grayson, a member of Jimmy's security detail, tackled the man. Another bodyguard rushed to the podium to cover Jimmy, and another guarded the entrance in case there were other threats.

Tyrone was a former detective with the Birmingham Police Department. He had no fat anywhere. He was muscle from head to toe. He was in his late forties, but he was still in excellent shape. At six foot five and nearly 250 pounds, he cast a big shadow. Tyrone knocked the wind out of the would-be assailant when he landed on him. The police were called and the man was arrested and booked.

Once the assailant's identity was confirmed, the connection to the infamous Percy Guthrie was undeniable. Brandon Kirkland was from Lamar County near Vernon. *Could this be an assignment issued by the white nationalist leader?* No one knew for sure then, but everybody was on edge after that episode.

The things Kirkland shouted in that room were deplorable, and Diane was depressed all the way home that night. She had heard boos and whispers of racist chants at other campaign stops, but nothing like the vitriol she witnessed that night.

The unveiled, naked hatred was unmistakable and real. It reminded the entourage just what kind of element they had awakened with Jimmy's notoriety. The ugly, terrible beast of racism had gone on the prowl in Tuscaloosa, and it would be a threat for the balance of the campaign.

Chapter 7

Sweet Land of Liberty

When we landed in Birmingham, Jimmy was very quiet as he reflected on what happened in Tuscaloosa.

The first thing that entered his mind was the terror he saw in Diane's face that night. "What gives anyone the right to say you can't run for this office or that office?" he shouted. "I'm a tax-paying, law-abiding citizen, and I will not be ordered around like a child. Who the devil do they think they are?"

Kirkland had threatened Jimmy and his entire family. He had called Diane horrible names and talked about burning down their home in Pelham. Kirkland boasted about knowing the addresses of Russell's home and business, Diane's workplace, Marsha's home and workplace, and Cliff's home and workplace. "How long had Kirkland watched the movements of our campaign?" he asked. "Are other people watching my family?"

Tyrone and another former law enforcement officer from the sheriff's department began a thorough investigation of the Guthrie clan. Riley Agee was six foot three and weighed 240 pounds, and he was a little rotund. He had been an expert marksman in the army, and his specialty was side arms. Using Agee's numerous contacts in law enforcement, they amassed quite a file on the group. They had names and photos of the ringleaders and placed calls to add security. The campaign was flush with cash and could easily afford to beef up the security detail.

Jimmy was furious about how his wife had been treated by what he called "vermin."

Diane looked at Jimmy and said, "Do you remember the *Daily Word* from last Friday that we discussed? Charles Fillmore said, 'Patience has its foundation in faith, and it is perfected only in those who have unwavering faith in God?' Jimmy, these people do not represent all the white folks in this state. They are unhappy, bitter people who want everyone else to be unhappy too. Don't worry about me. I can take it. I'll get over this horrible night."

It took Diane and Tyrone several minutes to calm Jimmy down. He could bear the insults and threats on himself, but he drew a firm line when it came to his wife. He would fight and die for her. Even with threats escalating, he asked for more exposure because he felt that he could win the nomination.

Diane cautioned him about going into certain areas.

Jimmy said, "Be strong and courageous. Do not be afraid or terrified because of them, for the Lord your God goes with you; he will never leave you nor forsake you. That's from Deuteronomy 31:6. I refuse to cower to those terrorists."

Jimmy would not let up. His aim was to stump up and down the state as he chose. The opportunity to win the nomination was there. Jimmy's organization was second to none. He had people who were dedicated to the campaign. Cleo Jones had done yeoman's work of raising funds and organizing supporters. Steven Poindexter was forming a powerful statewide coalition that was the envy of politicians everywhere.

Jimmy owed it to them to do his very best. His campaign would focus on north Alabama again. Jimmy had slight gains there in the polls. He needed to capitalize on that momentum. There was no time for trepidation or insecurity. It was on to Tuscumbia and Russellville. After stumping in those northwestern cities, Jimmy planned to hit Huntsville one more time before the primary.

Danger lurked in the northwestern part of the state, and hatred would again take center stage. Jimmy gave a rousing speech in Tuscumbia at the civic center.

While they were on their way to the Russellville Greystone Hotel Ballroom, Percy Guthrie was busy making plans of his own. The double-wide trailer was packed that morning. Percy had assembled one of the toughest bunch of thugs in the state's history. There were nationalists from Mississippi, Louisiana, and Georgia. The homegrown representatives were just as devoted to the cause of white power as any of the out-of-staters.

After finding out that sheriff's deputies and local police would beef up the protection detail for Russell's visit to Russellville, Percy toned down his original plan. He had planned to assassinate the African-American politician. He felt he had the firepower and manpower to do it, but the added security gave him second thoughts. Percy altered his plan and decided to send a group of hecklers to the rally. For the time being, the guns would stay holstered. Guthrie had developed a real, abiding hatred for Jimmy. His mind was working overtime about the best way to get at Russell.

The speech commenced at 6:45 that evening. The crowd was receptive, but a smattering of boos could be heard toward the back of the ballroom. At first, it didn't seem to be much of a problem—but the booing got louder and more people seemed to be joining in.

The security team started to fan out in the large room. Tyrone went directly to the back of the room. As soon as he approached a young man in army fatigues and a green T-shirt, the young nationalist pledge shouted, "Kill the nigger!"

Sheriff deputies converged around Jimmy at the podium. Tyrone grabbed the young man and pushed him toward the front entrance. Two more protesters circled Tyrone, pressed against him, and cursed him vehemently.

Agee rushed to Jimmy's defense and pulled out his pepper spray. The crowd had been directed to walk through metal detectors, so there was little concern about weapons being a threat, but people could be hurt if a brawl broke out.

People rushed toward the rear exit, and the rally was over, which was just what Percy wanted. Jimmy was hurried out the rear door by three deputies with their guns drawn. The local policemen in the detail ran outside to see to the safety of people leaving the rally.

Police escorted the car that ushered Jimmy to a hotel across town. Other officers were called to restore order and make necessary arrests. The amazing thing about the whole incident, according to Tyrone, was Jimmy's demeanor during the uproar. Russell displayed no emotion on his face. He was as cool as a guy at a church social. It struck me as odd also. With all the noise and chaos, Mr. Russell showed no emotion at all.

Jimmy said, "Tyrone, that whole thing had to have been orchestrated. Didn't it seem staged to you? If they wanted to hurt me, they probably could have."

"Boss, this thing is getting a little crazy," said Tyrone. "It seems to be building toward something."

"Yeah, that's my read too," Jimmy replied.

"The hate mail and the phone calls to the office are putting everybody on edge."

"Yeah, Mrs. Morris said the bag with the ugly letters is almost full," I added.

At the hotel, Jimmy called Diane. "Baby, they messed up my rally. They slipped a group into the meeting—and they tore the whole thing up."

"What did they do?" Diane asked.

"On top of the typical booing, they started to shout racist rants and all kinds of profanity. One of them screamed 'Kill the nigger!' People started to leave when the yelling started. Somebody is really out to get me, Di."

"Oh my God, Jimmy. Is it worth all of this?"

"Di, as shook up as I am, nobody must know. I still say that I have a right to run—and damn it, I'm gonna!"

Tyrone knocked on the door and said, "Is everything all right, Doc?"

"Yep, I'm just talking to Diane. I'm letting her know what those thugs did to my rally."

"Okay, Doc."

Jimmy said, "Di, I'm going to keep my appointment with the good people of Huntsville."

"I know you're not going to quit. I'll help you weather this storm. I'm going back on the trail with you. If you are going to face danger, I'll face it with you. I've worked in Birmingham to raise funds for your campaign. I've spoken in churches—black and white."

"But—"

"Laci and I did two interviews with the television stations to pitch your cause. The Tuscaloosa fiasco scared the daylights out of me. I had never seen such animosity up close and personal. It was raw, unabashed hatred in its purest form. It illustrated the real peril a political candidate can encounter when people lose control of their perspectives. That Guthrie gang has lost control. They are out for blood."

"What can we do, Di?"

"Let's focus on the good folks on the trail. There are some really good people in Alabama—and they deserve the best leadership. You are the leader Alabama needs. You'll be everybody's governor. You'll be there when they need you. Jimmy, you've always been a savior in crises. In an emergency, they call you because of your cool head and fierce loyalty. You have strength, conviction, and willpower. The things you believe in are what made you who you are. You are more than willing to take the consequences for holding to your beliefs—no matter how unpopular they are."

Mrs. Russell called Tyrone and told him about her plans to join her husband in Huntsville. Tyrone told a friend of his in Birmingham, an active officer on the police force, to serve as Mrs. Russell's bodyguard and chauffeur. Avery Smith, a former Alabama A&M football player, was a bodybuilder and amateur boxer. After Tyrone gave Avery directions to the hotel, he asked the officer to see if anyone else was interested in picking up some extra money as bodyguards. There was real danger in the air.

Poindexter put out the word that Jimmy's threat level had increased dramatically. This was an attempt to get the local authorities on board for Jimmy's protection. No one wanted to have the stain of having something happen to the lawyer from Birmingham on their watch.

It was an extremely important rally to swing some of the crucial white votes in north Alabama. Huntsville was the most populous city in the region and a veritable pipeline for campaign donations. Huntsville had become a progressive, bustling city, which was known for a lot more than the space industry. The stakes had never been higher, and people would watch closely for signs of troublemakers at the assembly.

A couple of off-duty troopers attended this meeting. Many people thought it was at the behest of the mayor. Tony Morrow was no fool. The mayor knew what the press would do to the reputation of his beloved city if Russell got hurt—or worse—there. The primary was just two weeks away, and Jimmy would look to eastern and southern Alabama to close out the campaign.

Once Diane arrived, Jimmy seemed to relish the thought of tackling the Democratic hard-liners in Huntsville—men who were as financially conservative as their Republican counterparts. Their views clashed with

Jimmy's on issues like welfare and Medicaid. But, as usual, Jimmy laid out his plan and didn't apologize for disagreeing with some of them.

They were important donors, but he could not and did not bend to their will.

Diane sat in the first row of the luxurious Capers Room at the Steadman's Suites Hotel and watched her husband deliver one of his best speeches. She noticed how smooth his delivery had become. His eye contact was much better when he spoke. He actually told a joke or two—and pulled them off quite well. The trip was made even more enjoyable because Christy Poindexter was there. It was on to points east!

Chapter 8

Win or Go Home!

The old sports adage "win or go home" couldn't have been more appropriate for this contest. The polls were still very tight between the top three contenders for the Democratic Nomination for governor.

One week, Jimmy held a two-point lead over Roberts, and Watkins was just a point off. Another week, Jimmy and Roberts would be in a virtual tie—and Watkins would be right behind them. For two weeks running, it was almost a dead heat between the three of them. It was going to be a nail-biting, photo-finish race, and everybody knew it. Curry had dropped out of the race the week before, and Floyd was polling in the low single digits.

Jimmy put the campaign in another gear and stumped harder than ever. One of the main targets for the Russell campaign for the last two weeks before the primary were the towns along the eastern border of the state.

In Dothan, Eufaula, Phenix City, Opelika, and Heflin, he had to win over some white voters. It was a must, and Poindexter knew it. He wasn't just thinking about the primary either. He had his eye on a much bigger prize. A place he knew very well from his time there: Montgomery.

Poindexter had confided to close friends that Jimmy had a legitimate shot at winning the whole thing. That was indeed a mouthful—considering the enormous challenge if he were to win the nomination—but Steven actually believed in taking things one step at a time. He felt that Jimmy had enough on his plate for the moment. Poindexter loved to talk about the evolution of his candidate. From the early days in north Alabama to the homestretch, he witnessed an amazing metamorphosis of a man.

He couldn't help but recall those careful, measured introduction speeches his candidate delivered in the beginning. To Poindexter, this was not the same man. Russell had matured as a speaker and as a politician. He was allowing his personality to shine. He was still a straightforward, no-nonsense guy, but a more engaging type of demeanor was on display. Steven thought this new version of James Russell would be tough to beat in any election.

Speaking in Dothan at the Belmont Country Club Grand Ballroom, he gave a speech on the need for real leadership in Montgomery. During the speech, Jimmy noticed the size and makeup of the crowd. The crowds were getting larger, and they were predominantly white.

He was thrilled to see the increased numbers of white voters coming to hear his speeches, but he wondered about the absence of the minority voters he depended on so much.

Poindexter was in the audience that day, and he talked to Jimmy after the speech. "Jimmy, don't worry. Most minority voters can't afford to come to a place like this."

Jimmy thought that Poindexter had made a good point. Jimmy thought that they better not take the minority vote for granted. He asked Poindexter to get his secretary to make some calls to black community leaders in Dothan. He also wanted black leaders contacted in the remaining cities they would visit in eastern Alabama.

Instead of speaking to white-dominated assemblies, the entourage would also swing through the black neighborhoods as well. Jimmy was polling very well with minority voters, but he had to have a massive turnout on Election Day. One of the things Poindexter worked so hard on was organizing the turnout efforts all over the state.

Turnout was paramount. As the campaign moved through east Alabama, nothing was left to chance. The appeal went out—from the candidate himself—for all registered Democrats to get out and vote.

The east Alabama circuit served the campaign well. The polls were showing slight leads for Jimmy, and the election would be held the following Tuesday. When the Heflin stop rolled around, Jimmy was worn out.

In his hotel room, Jimmy called his wife. "Di, I'm just beat. I wish this thing was over tomorrow. If I win, there's only more pressure waiting for me. Man, I need some rest."

"You can rest later. First, you have to win the nomination. That's what you've been fighting for, Jimmy—so finish it. Like Papa Henry used to say, 'Finish what you start.' It's time to man up!"

Jimmy said, "Okay, Coach! I'll close out the campaign in Birmingham and the surrounding area. It's time to energize the base and get out the home vote."

The home base was the most populous in the state. He had to make sure the organization in Jefferson County was working at 100 percent capacity.

Cleo Jones had his people out in force, lining up drivers to get folks to the polls. He had people handing out flyers all over the county and encouraging everyone to vote. Jimmy's face was plastered all over the county.

Jimmy had brief talks scheduled for several churches on the Sunday before the election. He stood in the audience, greeted everyone, and asked for their votes on Tuesday. It was on to the next stop and the next. The next day, he did interviews on television and on a black-owned radio station.

The big day was finally here. The election was at hand. Jimmy would pray and give the whole thing to God—the way he had with every other major event in his life. In spite of the insults, threats, harassing phone calls, hate mail, and disappointments, he stayed the course. You see, it was really important to him to complete the job.

Poindexter had reserved a suite of rooms at a Birmingham hotel for an election watch. Cleo Jones and his wife, Christy Poindexter, the core of Jimmy's security team and their spouses were invited to the watch. All of the attorneys in the firm and their wives were there as well as Russell's children and their spouses. I was there with my date, Kerri Ellis.

Poindexter had set out a spread to be revered. Mrs. Morris and her husband, James, were there also, and it was a night to remember. There was plenty of everything, and no one could have been more gracious than Steven Poindexter and his beautiful wife that night. He seemed to be happy and excited even before seeing any returns.

Diane and Christy got a chance to catch up, and then a hush came over the room. The results started to filter in, and Roberts had an early lead. The early vote tallies were coming in from west Alabama, especially the Tuscaloosa precincts. Roberts had led in that area since day one. Poindexter cautioned everyone not to worry. In the back of their minds, they all knew that Roberts would do all right in Jefferson County as well. Roberts was a native of Birmingham. While they were a little nervous, Jimmy was right on his heels. Watkins trailed by seven points early.

When the western Jefferson County precincts started to report, Jimmy began to close the gap with Roberts. When the tension in the room increased, Jimmy remained stoic and calm. He and Poindexter sat on a couch in front of the television and stared at the screen.

Others were seated around the bar or on chairs scattered throughout the spacious, luxury suite. Diane and Christy sat at a small table near the large television. Poindexter was very interested in seeing the north Alabama returns. He had spent a lot of time and money in that region and wanted to see results.

Jimmy pulled ahead at 9:30 when almost 70 percent of the precinct had reported. But, no one celebrated because Roberts had polled well in northeastern Alabama, which had only reported scant returns. As the returns from that region started to come in, everybody held their collective breaths. Roberts began to close the gap, and the election looked to be in peril for Jimmy.

When all seemed lost, a miraculous swing in the votes in Jackson County, in the northeastern corner of the state, started to report heavily in Jimmy's favor. Jimmy made an introductory speech there at the beginning of the campaign. They found out later that a real estate magnate named Dumas Rutledge saw Jimmy that day and liked what he had to say. He created his own organization to promote Jimmy for the nomination. These crucial votes and the eventual Mobile and Jefferson County margins won the election for James Earl Russell.

The room began celebrating when the anchorman said that James E. Russell of Birmingham had won the Democratic Nomination for governor of Alabama.

Russell hugged Diane, and everyone in the room congratulated him, wishing him well in the general election. Instead of shaking hands, Steven Poindexter walked up to Jimmy and embraced him like a brother. The two men had forged a strong bond during the campaign. His respect for Jimmy was unquestioned, and he really cared about him.

Tyrone Grayson had a tear in his eye because he knew what Russell had gone through. Tyrone walked over to Russell and said, "Boss, you did it."

Over everybody's congrats, Horace said, "Russ, you made history here tonight! Thank God I got to see it!"

Before the party was over, thoughts turned toward the general election. The incumbent governor would really be a handful! Zach Preston was an Alabama football legend. He lettered four years in Tuscaloosa and had a brief stint in the pros. His approval rating was in the sixties, and he had people lining up to get his autograph. He was a native of Mobile, and his wife had been a Miss Alabama contestant. Preston even had some Democrats backing his initiatives in the statehouse. All of the wealthy Republican donors would fill his war chest for the general election. An uphill battle awaited the Democrats—and that was well understood.

Jimmy didn't have much time to celebrate his victory or get any rest. There was a challenge of epic proportion for the man from Whitney. A party-strategy conference was planned for the following Tuesday in Gulf Shores. The hotel was right on the Gulf of Mexico, a beautiful spot with gorgeous, pristine beaches. The Democrats would plan their assault on the GOP. Since Republicans had been in power, gerrymandering had ruled the day in Montgomery. They were assured blocks of votes in certain districts, and the Democrats had little chance of breaking their stranglehold on these areas. The Democrats were ready for a fight. It had been almost a generation since a Democrat occupied the governor's mansion in Montgomery.

Poindexter asked Jimmy to bring Diane if she could get a substitute for her class. He said Christy wanted to go to enjoy the fantastic shopping in the area. The place had some of the best restaurants in Alabama. The seafood there was legendary.

Jimmy thought it would be a good place to escape some of the pressure he had felt for the past few months. Diane was able to clear her schedule for the four-day trip—and it gave her an opportunity to rewind too. She was just as invested in the campaign as Jimmy, and she needed a break from the unyielding action.

All the heavy hitters in the party would be there. Jimmy would need to rally his troops and get everybody on the same page. He would deliver an acceptance speech at the conference and lay out his plan for the campaign.

Steven called Professor Merrill and asked him to meet Jimmy in Birmingham and draft a speech for the conference. The professor agreed to meet Jimmy on the Thursday before the conference. That speech would be critical to the success of mobilizing all the assets in the party.

The Democrats had not been organized or galvanized in recent statewide elections. The time for splintered efforts and missed opportunities was over. If the Democrats had any chance of winning this election, there had to be complete solidarity in the party. It was Jimmy's job to get this done. He understood his role now: party leader. He was it. There was no one else to lean on for leadership. The party nominee was in charge, and by that time, Mr. Russell had grown into the role.

Jimmy had to assure the folks that they were in good hands with his lead. The country boy from Whitney was in high cotton, indeed. Strangely enough, he wasn't nervous about the upcoming conference. He was anxious, but there was no apprehension. A lot of it had worn away during the nomination campaign. He felt like a grizzled veteran.

The phone in the office in Birmingham was flooded with calls congratulating Jimmy on his victory. It was a historic occasion, but Jimmy's focus was on Gulf Shores! Not surprisingly, business had picked up since Jimmy's run for the governorship. Horace had covered for his pal admirably. The firm was doing quite well, and new business was not a problem.

On Thursday, Dr. Merrill arrived at the Sheraton Hotel in Birmingham at ten o'clock. He called Jimmy's office to ask him to come by the hotel restaurant for lunch. Once the two men finished their lunches, they went up to Merrill's room to work on the speech. The night before, Merrill had written out a draft to review with Jimmy. The professor had been careful to craft a motivational speech that would inspire and energize.

Jimmy made several suggestions for phrases he thought were important to include in the speech. They labored over the speech for more than three hours that day. Then, as was the professor's normal practice, he asked Jimmy to rehearse it in front of him. Jimmy would read the speech and place emphasis where needed and use variations in tone. It reminded him of the public speaking class at 'Bama State. He remembered Greenlea talking about enunciation and intonation during that memorable semester.

When they finished polishing and tweaking the speech, Jimmy said, "Thanks and so long, Dr. Merrill."

Before Jimmy walked out, Merrill said, "Mr. Russell, you've got my vote."

Russell looked squarely into Merrill's eyes and said, "That means a lot to me, Doc." Russell had nothing but respect for the middle-aged, heavyset man. He had learned so much about the fine art of public speaking from a man who had devoted much of his life to the language arts. The men had exchanged cell numbers long ago, and Russell felt comfortable calling Merrill anytime for advice.

Chapter 9

Fight to the Finish

On Monday evening, Tyrone pulled up in front of Russell's Pelham home. He was there to drive the couple to the airport for the flight to Jack Edwards Airport. In Gulf Shores, they would register at the hotel the night before the conference. This would allow time for Russell and Diane to have a nice meal with Steven and Christy. After settling in the hotel and relaxing from the flight, the couples—plus their security detail—went to one of the area's nicest seafood restaurants. Jimmy loved his seafood. The food was excellent, and the four people had come to really enjoy each other's company.

More than three hundred miles to the northwest, Percy Guthrie was having a meal in the double-wide with four of his friends. Percy had read, with great interest, about Russell's trip to Gulf Shores. Already fuming over Russell's win in the Democratic nomination, Percy was coiled and ready to strike. They discussed borrowing camera equipment from friends in Huntsville. What in the world would Percy Guthrie want with camera equipment? Percy planned to use two of his most devoted followers to try to kill Jimmy Russell.

The conference was big news, and Guthrie thought that security might be lax in that kind of setting. He needed two shooters to pose as cameramen and get close enough to gun Jimmy down. The assassins had to know that the risk to their own lives was pretty grave. These guys were just the type of fanatics Percy needed for this assignment. To bring down a black man who was seeking the highest office in Alabama would be crowning achievement for those kind of true believers.

The clean-shaven, neatly dressed, and well-mannered men would be driven to the front of a jewelry store next to the hotel to await Russell's scheduled press conference. They were to blend in with the throng of reporters and cameramen in front of the beautiful hotel.

The car would wait for them behind the jewelry store after the hit. They knew their chances of making it to the car were slim to none. The men knew that state troopers, deputy sheriffs, local policemen, and private security would be in close proximity to Russell during the press briefing. The two nationalists from Mississippi were devout white supremacists. They were not afraid to die for their beliefs. Both men were in their twenties, and they looked no different from many of the photographers who would be in attendance that day.

The morning of the conference was a clear, sunny day. Sixty-eight degrees was not bad for March weather on the Gulf. People were milling around the shops in the massive hotel lobby or eating breakfast at one of the hotel's restaurants. Scores of hotel guests were walking on the beach that morning. Couples were always walking up and down the broad sidewalk in front of the numerous hotels that lined the avenue.

It looked like a glorious day for the Democrats to get their show on the road. It would be a great kickoff to what they hoped was a winning strategy for the campaign. At 8:50, Russell and Diane emerged from their room. Tyrone, Riley, and Avery were working the security detail.

I was already in the lobby, waiting for the news conference to begin. I had slept so well the night before, and the breakfast was delicious. Our spacious rooms opened to balconies that looked right into the Gulf of Mexico. It was absolutely awesome.

When they reached the lobby, Christy, Steven, and Cleo Jones were waiting by the podium. Others were waiting in the lobby. The local newspapers and television stations had representatives there to cover the event. Media outlets from Mobile, Montgomery, Tuscaloosa, Anniston, and Birmingham attended the event.

At 9:15, Russell followed his security detail through the glass doors and walked up to the podium. Diane was slightly behind and to the right of Jimmy.

Poindexter and Christy stood behind and to his left. Tyrone and Riley were beside him. The troopers were to their front and sheriff's deputies were watching the glass doors behind the group. Police officers were positioned on the sidewalk in front of hotel.

Just as Russell was saying good morning, Tyrone saw a man raise a weapon, leaped in front of Jimmy, and shouted "Gun!," then several shots rang out. People ran for cover. At least eight shots were heard and then more shots followed. The assassins had gotten off several shots before they were gunned down. The policemen near the sidewalk saw the shooters and shot and killed them, but the horror had just begun. By the podium, a trooper had a bullet wound to his lower leg. A sheriff's deputy was on his back and had a gunshot wound to his abdomen.

Russell looked down and saw Tyrone on the pavement. "Call 911! Somebody call 911!" he yelled.

Everybody was rushing to aid the injured or calling for help.

Russell looked around to see if Diane was all right. He didn't see her at first, but when he looked down, Diane was on the ground—and bleeding profusely from her shoulder and back.

Christy was helping Diane sit up. Christy had blood all over her dress and her face.

Jimmy immediately got down on his knees and placed his handkerchief over her wound.

Diane was semiconscious and groaning.

Jimmy felt totally helpless and shouted, "Oh my God! Please get help!!"

Tyrone was in a pool of blood. A bullet had struck his neck, severing his carotid artery.

The paramedics arrived, and people were treated and transported to emergency rooms.

The authorities roped off the scene with police tape, and people were asked to leave the immediate area.

When one of the paramedics got to Tyrone, he looked over at Mr. Russell and said, "I'm sorry. He didn't make it."

The medical examiner rushed over to Tyrone and pronounced him dead. When Jimmy saw the terrible wound to Tyrone's neck, he knew the bullet was meant for him. I can't describe the sickening feeling I experienced that fateful morning. All of the blood, people running for cover, the screaming and crying; it was one of the most awful scenes I have witnessed in my life. I was standing just three feet behind Mrs. Russell when she was hit. I saw her slump to the ground and Christy reaching over to try and break her fall. We both tried to sit her up and I called out to Mr. Russell to get his attention. He was busy looking after

Tyrone in front of the podium. The whole scene was like something out of a war movie.

While the police officers were taking statements, Jimmy and I got into an ambulance with Diane. Gulf Shores police and state troopers escorted us to the hospital. Mrs. Russell would open her eyes briefly and doze off again, which really scared me.

At the emergency room, Russell called Pastor Lawrence to ask him for a favor. He asked Reverend Lawrence to drive to Roger's Elementary School and break the news about Tyrone's death to Tina Grayson. She was the school secretary. Russell could not allow her to hear it from a newscast.

Lawrence said, "We'll be praying for Tyrone's family and Diane's recovery."

After thanking Lawrence, he called Laci and Cliff to tell them about the shooting. He asked Laci to call her aunt Marsha and break the tragic news to her. Marsha was shocked and immediately started making plans to travel to Gulf Shores.

Laci was hysterical, and Jimmy had to plead with her to remain calm.

Not wanting to wait on an afternoon flight, Cliff, Laci, Marsha, and Horace left Birmingham in Craig's SUV.

Craig said that Marsha prayed silently during the trip down I-65. Laci was really out of it. She would cry and then stare out the window. Cliff was quiet but just as worried as the women.

Horace pushed the Cadillac Escalade at ninety miles per hour down the road.

Russell told everyone about the severity of the wound and that the damage was done by a .357 Magnum. The bullet that struck Diane's shoulder entered into the subscapularis muscle tissue and took a slightly upward trajectory. It then smashed into the acromioclavicular joint, causing terrible damage. All the way to the hospital, she was in and out of consciousness.

Russell prayed and held her hand tightly as the ambulance sped toward the hospital. At the hospital, the policemen formed a protective shield around the couple. Christy had insisted on going to the hospital, but Steven finally persuaded her to at least change clothes before going.

The two shooters had not been identified yet, but law enforcement suspected Percy was behind it. The weapons were going be processed through ballistics, and the serial numbers would be traced. Everything was being done to establish a motive for the crime. *Who paid for the expensive camera equipment they carried? Who supplied the guns and ammunition? Was Jimmy Russell the target? How did they get to the hotel?*

All these questions had to be answered, but Diane's health was all that mattered to Jimmy. Without her, none of the other things were of consequence. Jimmy wanted his wife to be all right again.

At the hospital, Jimmy learned that the sheriff's deputy, Todd Brewster, had died. The bullet had creased his liver, and they lost him in the ambulance. Jimmy was sad beyond description. His life had been turned upside down. His wife was on an operating table, and his good friend was dead. Another good man had lost his life in defense of his. He felt a tremendous amount of guilt because of this. He asked at the nurse's station where to find the chapel and was directed there by an aide. Avery and Riley went with him. Riley was wiping away tears, and Avery had water welling up in his eyes.

"God, I can't believe that Ty is gone," Riley said.

"He was a good man … the best. Would give you the shirt off his back," Avery said.

"Let's pray for his and the deputy's families," Jimmy said.

We all prayed and fought back tears as Jimmy prayed aloud. I really liked Mr. Grayson.

At seven thirty that night, Laci, Cliff, Marsha, and Horace arrived at the hospital. Laci embraced her dad and sobbed. Cliff wrapped his arms around both them and asked about his mom's condition. Marsha wanted to know if her sister's life was in danger. Horace embraced his friend and told him he was really sorry about everything.

Russell said, "The surgeon came out about an hour ago and said her condition was upgraded to stable. When we arrived at the hospital, she was classified as critical, which frightened me something fierce."

"Daddy, is Mama going to be all right? I mean, what about the use of her right arm?" Cliff asked.

"I don't know, Cliff. They haven't really broken that down for me yet," Jimmy responded.

"God, Daddy! Tyrone is dead! I can't believe it. He was like part of the family," said Laci.

"I know Tyrone looked up to you like a father. Daddy, he loved you," Cliff said.

"I cared a lot about that boy. He was some man. The last thing he did was save my life," Russell said, shaking his head.

"Hey! You can't feel guilty about that. Tyrone was trying to do his job. We will always be grateful for what he did, but we have to go on," Laci said.

At ten o'clock, the doctor came back out. The surgery was over, and Diane was resting comfortably. A nurse would notify them when they could see her. Jimmy wanted to know more about the damage to her shoulder and the use of her arm.

The surgeon said that the damage was extensive—and more surgery might be needed—but they were more concerned at the moment with getting her stabilized. Once she was strong enough, further surgeries might be prescribed. We were all thankful that she was alive.

Back at the hotel, everything was a mess. The Democrats were in total disarray. Some members were preparing to leave, thinking the conference would be canceled, but Poindexter and his secretary were working feverishly to hold things together.

Cleo Jones arrived at the hospital at ten thirty to check on Diane. He said that party members had vowed to stay in spite of the chaos.

Steven called and said, "Jimmy, I have an idea that might work. Why don't I come to the hospital, give you a change of clothes, and have you videotape the speech? The speech can be played on the big screen in the ballroom. The other parts of the conference can resume as scheduled. You won't have to leave Diane's side at all."

Steven and Christy brought the clothes and his briefcase. One of the hotel geeks followed them to the hospital with the taping machinery.

Jimmy thought the idea was fine, but he needed to take a shower and relax before taping the speech.

Poindexter talked a resident physician into letting Russell use the shower in his office. Poindexter wrote the book on thinking on your feet.

At about midnight, Jimmy went into the hospital chapel to tape the speech, which meant so much to so many people.

Since the lighting was poor in the chapel, Poindexter borrowed some of the lamps in the waiting room. Once the lighting was suitable, the taping could begin. There was a small lectern in the corner. It was moved to the center of the room.

After greeting the assembly, he started the speech with a quote by Thomas Edison. "Our greatest weakness lies in giving up. The most certain way to succeed is always to try just one more time." He updated the group about his wife's condition and expressed his deep sorrow for the loss of the two brave men who fell that day. He asked for prayers for their families and prayers for the officer who was wounded.

After a brief pause, he said, "The people who thought this act would stop my drive toward Montgomery were sadly mistaken. Let me share a quote from Arthur Ashe. 'Start where you are. Use what you have. Do what you can.' Republican money and dirty tricks cannot stop the force of determined, focused Democrats. The goal is to fight to the end … no matter what. There will be no letting up, no backing down, and no compromising. Bullets won't stop me, and insults are fuel for my fire. I'll close my speech with a quote from the late Maya Angelou. 'We may encounter many defeats, but we must not be defeated.'"

When I saw him deliver that speech, my chest was bursting with pride. Being a witness to the events of that day changed my life forever.

Chapter 10

The Homestretch

Diane was hospitalized for a week in Gulf Shores. Jimmy only left to attend Tyrone's funeral. Marsha stayed in Gulf Shores while Jimmy was away that day.

Jimmy made phone calls, and surrogates made speeches in his stead. He couldn't leave Diane down there alone. Cliff and Laci had to get back to work after seeing their mom and feeling she was out of danger.

While Jimmy was in Gulf Shores, the funeral for Officer Brewster was scheduled for 11am on Friday in Mobile, his hometown. Jimmy attended the funeral and had a chance to speak to Brewster's widow. Jimmy was really pleased to see the outpouring of support shown to the Brewster family.

Grayson's funeral was scheduled for Saturday at eleven o'clock in Birmingham. Jimmy and the entire family, except Marsha, attended Tyrone's funeral. Jimmy delivered the eulogy and fought back tears the whole while. He often said that it was one of the toughest things he ever had to do. Half of the Birmingham Police Department was there, and representatives from several suburban police forces were present too. Tyrone Grayson was honored for the man he was.

Meanwhile, things were heating up for Percy and the crew. Once pictures showing the carnage in Gulf Shores went viral on social media and were plastered on the front pages of newspapers across the country, a cry went out for justice. The police knew they didn't have any concrete evidence that Percy had ordered the attack, but one of his underlings might break and give him up if they worked them hard enough.

Surveillance was placed on two minions in particular. Percy's cousin, Stony Cargill, was an extremely talkative person. Once Stony had enough corn whiskey in him, you couldn't stop him from talking.

Reggie Farris was an ex-con and a long-time nationalist. Reggie had terrible financial troubles, and the police could use inducements of money to try to get him to talk.

Eventually, Stony cracked under the pressure. He gave his cousin up for a reduced sentence on a robbery charge. That was just the tip of the iceberg. Two other nationalists from Georgia came forward with testimony against Percy Guthrie. When all was said and done, Percy got life without the possibility of parole. The two assassins in the Gulf Shores rampage were later identified as Damon Crews and Searcy Crews, first cousins and suspected multiple murderers.

Alabama has its share of racism, like any other state in this union, but this shooting angered a lot of white folks. People being shot down in broad daylight without a care who the bullets struck was just too much for the average Alabamian. Something had to be done. An active sheriff's deputy and a former police detective were dead; someone had to pay.

When Diane arrived at her home in Pelham, all kind of cards and flowers were placed on the front porch by well-wishers. This really lifted her spirits, and the road to her rehabilitation was made that much easier.

Her shoulder was absolutely stiff and painful at times. She tried to stay off painkillers as much as possible, fearing addiction. She missed her kids at college, but her health was the important thing now. She was scheduled for an examination at University Hospital to determine the best course of action for her treatment. Her doctor was a renowned specialist from Atlanta, Dr. Phillip Nabors.

Meanwhile, as the gubernatorial campaign entered the summer months, strange things started to happen in the polls. Right after Jimmy's nomination, the lead that Preston enjoyed was in the double digits. But Russell got a sympathy bump, and he was only nine points behind.

The Democrats had to seize this chance. Maybe Preston wasn't invincible. But, as July turned to August, the gap was still eight points; something had to be done. Two debates were scheduled, but Preston declined the invitation for a second debate. He claimed it was customary to have only one debate. The Democrats attacked him on that issue furiously, saying that he feared facing Jimmy.

Preston was no slouch behind the podium. He had warded off two very strong challengers for the Republican nomination. It was a little arrogant to think that this experienced, confident man was afraid of Jimmy. Or was he?

The debate was scheduled for August 15, which gave Jimmy a little time to get ready. He called Professor Merrill to collaborate on a strategy, and they met in July. Jimmy devoted most his time to Diane and the campaign—in that order.

From his run toward the nomination, Jimmy knew which parts of the state he needed to work the most. He felt that the west-central area, including Tuscaloosa, was a definite target. He reached out to Roberts since his old rival had won the vote in that area by a wide margin in the primary.

Roberts contacted several supporters in Tuscaloosa and Greene Counties to enlist their help with Jimmy's campaign. Roberts and Jimmy had mutual respect for one another. Were they close? No. But they were both Democrats, and the goal was to kick the Republicans out of the governor's mansion.

The Democrats were practical when it came to counting on west-central Alabama for votes. This was definitely Preston country. The best the Democrats could hope for would be a 20 percent share of the vote there. Their motto was: No backing down, no giving up, and no compromising. We'll fight to the end.

Jimmy repeated that slogan in all of his newsletters. He sounded more and more like a Southern Baptist preacher. He said, "Maybe they needed a good sermon to get them in gear."

West Alabama was only one part of the state. Jimmy had his eyes on some juicy prizes in the populous areas of the state. He knew he would have to really pummel Preston in Jefferson, Madison, Mobile, Etowah, and Shelby Counties to stand a chance in the election. He knew Preston would win the rural vote, and the only way to offset that was by winning the metro vote convincingly.

After consulting with Dr. Merrill, Jimmy hit the road. Diane wanted it that way. She wanted him to do everything he could to help change the direction of the state. He campaigned hard in west Alabama. He made the usual swing through north Alabama, and then to east

Alabama—the same way he had done it in the primary. He missed Tyrone a lot as he journeyed through these familiar places. No one could really replace Tyrone. Russell would never forget him.

The debate was held at the Montgomery Civic Center in the eastern part of town. The large stage was an imposing sight. The moderator sat off to right of the two men. Dr. Claudia Landis was a professor in the social science department at Tuskegee University. The two men struggled with the gay marriage question, but they both shined on the taxation issue—no matter how far apart their views were. The immigration debate was very heated, and Preston was visibly angry during one exchange. He had always been known for his cool demeanor, but not that night.

When it came to charter schools and public education, the heat was turned up once more. Preston was agitated again. Russell had always championed public education, and Preston was a big supporter of charter schools.

This segment of the debate illustrated just how far apart the two were on some of the state's hottest issues. Voters had two distinct choices in this election. Gun control, which always brought out the crazies in Alabama, was the last issue debated—and it was very contentious. Jimmy was for stricter gun control, and Preston was just the opposite. Neither man gave an inch.

When the debate ended, the men shook hands and forced smiles. Many called it a draw, but Democrats called it a resounding victory because a draw with Preston was definitely a win. The Montgomery newspaper called it a "bare-knuckle fistfight." Another paper said the two men "slugged it out for ten rounds." The Democrats pointed to their candidate's cool demeanor as testament of his self-control and poise under fire.

In late September, a story broke in an Anniston newspaper about a twenty-two-year-old coed who claimed to be Zach Preston's mistress. He denied the assertion, but it got people talking and investigating.

The reporter who broke the story said that there was evidence of an affair. Wow! Everybody was talking about the story—just before the election too! Preston did interview after interview to try to kill this story, but the reporter had hotel receipts and security photos of the governor leaving a hotel and the young lady leaving soon after.

Preston confessed to the "fling" and apologized. Many Republicans believed the Democrats had paid Shelley Hatcher, a journalism major, to come forward. She denied taking money from anyone. She said she was angry with the governor because of broken promises. Miss Hatcher would never say publicly what those promises were.

As popular as Preston was, he thought people would forgive him. The Democratic camp was thrilled about the opening the Republican Party had given them on a platter. The Democrats believed this really opened the door.

Russell did not gloat; he kept working and tending to his wife. Every morning when he was in town, he made Diane go through her exercises. The doctor decided not to perform surgery and gave her a rehabilitation plan.

Jimmy had a great month in the polls. The gap had narrowed to four points, which was within the margin of error. The affair definitely hurt Preston. No Democrat had posed a threat like that in years. All the Democrats could do was close extremely strong—and pray the voters turned out in huge numbers.

Christy and Steven visited Diane several times in Birmingham to see how she was doing. Christy and Diane's friendship served them well during the tough times.

With the election looming, Democrats across the state were feeling hopeful. They had a great candidate, a war chest bulging at the seams, and a turnout machine that was ready to go.

Poindexter went back to town for the election. He and Christy reserved the same suite from the primary election. They invited other Democrats to share the evening with them.

Diane and Jimmy arrived at the hotel around six o'clock as precinct reporting began.

Cleo sat next to the TV. He was glued to that set and forgot that his wife was alone by the bar. Preston was racking up the rural vote, as expected, but Jimmy's totals were holding firm in the metropolitan areas.

At ten thirty, things started to tighten up. Folks in the room could sense a shift in the returns. The Democrats had turned out in big numbers all over the state. The possibility of a Democrat winning the governor's race was real.

The anchorman for KLAX said, "Wait, we're going to call the governor's race in favor of James E. Russell, a Birmingham attorney. It is one of the closest elections in the past fifty years."

A thunderous yell went up in the room, and folks thought Cleo would have a heart attack.

Poindexter and Jimmy were jumping up and down and shouting, "We did it!"

Even Diane was yelling and pumping her left fist. It was a glorious night for a political party that had been downtrodden for a generation.

I walked over to Mr. Russell, grabbed his hand, and said, "Boss, you have given all of us a reason to laugh tonight."

"Larry, you've been a blessing for this campaign. Thank you for all of your hard work," he said.

That meant a lot to me. This great man thinking that I made difference was reward enough for me.

It was time to celebrate a new beginning. No one thought about the historic significance of Jimmy's election. The emphasis was placed on what the victory meant for the state of Alabama. No one really thought much about the race issue then. The Democrats were back in the governor's mansion.

It was hard to believe that it was even possible, but many factors played a part in this monumental upset. First, Democrats were able to match the GOP fund-raising apparatus. Next, the debate showed that Preston was indeed human. Another factor was the incredible turnout the Democrats engineered. Finally, the September scandal affected the race more than Republicans figured it would. I think that Jimmy campaigned harder than Preston. Russell never let up.

I was so proud of what Jimmy accomplished that election season. Sure, a black man won the race for governor of Alabama for the first time, but the source of my pride goes much deeper. I saw him as a shining example of what a man can be if he holds on to his principles— no matter what. Because of him, I learned to take criticism and grow from it. I have set standards for myself and my family.

I know how to work because I witnessed his labors and the tireless way he forged ahead. Jimmy Russell is a man—in every sense of the word. He doesn't bend with the first wind that comes along or allow pressure to compromise his integrity.

Through his tireless efforts as governor, Medicaid was expanded to include thousands more Alabama citizens. His work to improve the infrastructure in this state was extremely important. The educational initiatives he proposed, which were eventually passed by Congress, promoted public education. His fair taxation policies passed—after a protracted battle with some entrenched elements of the Republican Party. His efforts to remedy the terrible immigration policies of the previous administration, unfortunately, were not overturned during his term in office.

Most importantly, Russell proved to be a governor for all of Alabama's citizens. When it was time to file papers for a run at reelection, Russell refused to seek another term. He was determined to spend more time with his family. At age sixty-seven, he wanted to continue his law practice and spend time with the grandchildren.

Diane recovered most of the function in her right shoulder. On occasion, she still has stiffness, and she can only raise her right arm so far. She returned to teach at the junior college and became a popular public speaker. Diane and Christy have stayed in touch with one another. They are very close.

Steven and Jimmy maintained the bond they formed during the campaign. Jimmy has always given Steven credit for the success he enjoyed in the campaign. Steven continued to help Jimmy while he was governor. Steven Poindexter had contacts all over this state. He knew people in Congress who could help the governor get things done. Jimmy even had Steven on speed dial—wouldn't you?

Jimmy Russell made history in this state, but he'll be remembered for his genuine character. Unlike most politicians, he is a real, authentic straight shooter. You can trust what he says. If he can't do something, he'll say it. If he disagrees with something, he'll say it. If it's wrong, he'll say it's wrong.

As far as I am concerned, Jimmy Russell knew how to finish well—and his life is a testament to what faith can do in the humblest of God's creatures. Love conquers all.